12 LIFE'S INTERSECTION STORIES

AROONACHALUM

Contents

CHAPTER I

HAPPY NEW YEAR 2020

(This story takes place from December 31, 2018, to 2020)

(This story takes place from December 31, 2018, to 2020)

Aroon, a boy who had lived in the orphanage since childhood due to having no parents, was in his final year of B.A. studies at a government college with low tuition fees. John, the caretaker and father figure of the orphanage, was 85 years old. He had been running the orphanage for over 25 years with the help of donations and was known for his kindness toward all the children. Among them, he had a special fondness for Aroon because Aroon was both a good student and a kind-hearted person. Aroon shared everything with John, as he had no one else to talk to, and the bond between them was powerful.

On December 31, 2018, John arranged a New Year's party for the kids. Aroon had a question that had been on his mind since childhood, but he had never asked it. Feeling that this was the right time, Aroon finally asked, "Why do we celebrate this useless New Year?"

John was shocked to hear this and responded, "Why are you asking such a thing?"

Aroon replied, "We do the same things every year, and nothing ever changes in our lives. So why should we celebrate the New Year?"

John answered, "People celebrate events in life to welcome new things. They often stay awake until midnight for three occasions: 1) their birthday, 2) their wedding day, and 3) New Year's Eve. While birthdays and wedding days are personal celebrations, New Year's is the one event celebrated worldwide. People believe that each New Year brings a chance for improvement and change."

Aroon then asked, "Why don't we celebrate our birthdays?"

John replied, "Because we don't know all your exact birth dates here. So, take the New Year as our shared birthday and do your best in life."

He continued, "You say nothing changes every year. Here is your challenge. Start writing a personal diary from tomorrow and continue for the next year. On December 31, 2019, please show me the changes. I'm telling you, you'll face many changes—some good, some bad. Some will move you forward, some backwards. But in the end, the result will be positive."

After that conversation, they celebrated the arrival of 2019.

Aroon immediately accepted the challenge and began writing his diary.

In **January**, we celebrated the New Year joyfully. Everything in my life seemed normal at first. So, he asked John, "Nothing has changed yet." John replied with a question: "What did you eat yesterday & today, and what colour clothes did you wear?"

Aroon answered, "Yesterday I wore my favourite colour, but today I wore something different. Yesterday I didn't eat because it was non-vegetarian, but today I ate a full meal because it was my favourite food."

John smiled and said, "That's a small change. If you believe, you'll begin to feel the changes. Life doesn't change in one day—it's a slow process."

Later that month, Aroon learned that he was eligible to vote in the central government election. It made me happy because, for the first time after turning 18, he could vote.

In **February**, their orphanage management decided to merge with another orphanage due to the rising costs and a low number of children. From that merger, he developed a strong friendship with Anu, a girl from the other orphanage. She was also in her final year, studying Entertainment and Tourism Management at a government college, like him. They quickly became close friends and shared everything that happened in their lives. After the merge, their orphanage looked livelier and more beautiful.

In **March** was a joyful month— Aroon enjoyed both college and orphanage life. Their college held campus interviews, and he got a job offer from a small-scale business. They told him that he could join after his final exams.

One day, Anu told him, "Two weeks ago, when I was returning from college, I saw an old man who had fallen on the road. I gave him water and asked for his name and why he was alone. He didn't say much—just that his name was Raj and he liked taking evening walks. Today I saw him again and smiled at him. He smiled back, but still didn't say anything else about himself."

Aroon said, "Anu, not everyone is as friendly as you. Just let it go and focus on your own life."

In **April**, he had my final exams. He studied very well, but unfortunately failed one subject. He was feeling low and sat quietly in my room. John came in and asked what was wrong, so he told him.

John reminded him that he told you that sometimes you will go backwards."

Aroon asked, "But how did I go backwards?"

John explained, "You studied but didn't pass. Now you'll need to retake that paper next month, while your friends are moving ahead. That's going backwards. But if you score 90% next time, it will be even better."

That made me reflect and feel more at peace.

Later, Anu told him that she had tried to learn more about Raj. She had followed him one day and found out he was staying at a retirement home. She asked the staff why he was there, but they didn't give her any details. Aroon said, "Oh, okay."

In **May**, Aroon cleared the arrears paper and joined my new job. he started learning many new things about how real life works in the workplace. Anu encouraged me, and Aroon told her everything that was happening in my office.

One day, Anu told him, "Raj called me and asked why I came to the retirement home and inquired about him. She told him it was just curiosity, and he got emotional. He then invited her for a cup of coffee and shared his life story with her. He said he had one son and lost his wife shortly after their child was born. He raised his son well, but once his son grew up and moved to the USA for work, he never came back. Eventually, his son placed him in a retirement home. Raj said he found peace seeing others like him and accepted his situation."

Anu continued, "I asked him how they spend their time in the home. Raj said, 'In the mornings, we do our chores like washing clothes, bathing, watching TV, and reading newspapers. In the evenings, we take walks. When we return, we share our unique talents."

Then Anu said to Aroon,
" When Raj shared his story, I felt that although we grew up without parents, we always wished we had them. But people like Raj are being abandoned by their children. That's even more painful."

Aroon replied, "This is the kind of world we live in. Some things can't be changed."

Anu didn't like Aroon's reply, but she didn't show her feelings to Aroon at that time.

After that, Anu avoided meeting Raj out of sadness. Life continued as usual.

In **June**, Aroon received his first salary. He bought treats for the children in the orphanage and donated the remaining money to the orphanage management. When John heard this, he asked, "Why are you doing this? Why didn't you save some money for yourself?"

Aroon replied, "This orphanage raised me to be a good human being. Why shouldn't I contribute back? You know what I need better than I do, so I trust you'll use it wisely."

Hearing this, John became emotional and said, "I've found the right person to look after this orphanage after I'm gone."

Aroon asked him, "Why are you saying things like that?"

John replied, "It's a fact—one day, everyone must leave this world."

Aroon said, "Father, please think positively."

John smiled, "Okay, let's see what happens."

But in **July**, John passed away due to his age. Everyone was heartbroken. Though the orphanage management continued their duties, the children slowly returned to normal. But Aroon couldn't recover. Aroon lost focus at work, and Anu tried to comfort me, but he remained in grief.

In **August**, Raj met Anu and asked why she had been avoiding him. Anu said, "I feel bad because I couldn't do anything for you."

Raj replied, "People who are in my situation only need someone to talk to us. To forget our loneliness, because "Loneliness is painful."

Hearing this, Anu said, "Grandpa, I will be with you from now on."

Tears welled up in Raj's eyes. Anu asked, "Why are you crying?"

He answered, "You're the first person to call me 'Grandpa.'"

Anu asked, "Can I call you like that?"

Raj replied, "Of course, my grandchild."

They were both happy.

On the same day, Aroon's boss, Bala, called him and asked, "Aroon, what's wrong with you? Why aren't you performing well?"

He told him everything about John, his past, and his emotions.

Bala said, "It's okay, Aroon. Try to forget it."

Then he asked, "Do you know why I hired you?"

Aroon said, "No."

Bala replied, "When I saw your resume, I saw that you grew up without parents, just like me. I was also an orphan. I studied hard and achieved my position after 20 years of struggle. My wife loved me even before I had anything. Now, we have money and assets, but no children. I helped you because I know that pain."

Aroon said, "You and John are both role models for me."

Bala replied, "I'll support you just like John did. Think of me as your brother."

Those words brought him back to life.

That night, Anu and Aroon discussed everything that had happened. I told her, "It's okay to talk to Raj—he's a good person."

She replied, "Hmm."

In **September**, things started to improve. Anu got a job at an entertainment firm as a Master of Ceremonies (MC). That day, she brought sweets to everyone in the orphanage.

That night, she sent a message on WhatsApp, proposing marriage. But he didn't reply. Even after that, Aroon continued speaking to her normally, which left her confused.

In **October**, an economic crisis affected the entire world. Bala gathered all employees and announced, "From next month, our office may shut down. Please start looking for new jobs."

But Aroon refused to leave him alone. Aroon told him, "You supported me when I needed it the most. Now it's my turn to stand by you. Whatever happens, we'll face it together." Bala accepted his offer.

Meanwhile, Anu visited the retirement home and gave sweets from her first month's salary. She quickly became a favourite among the residents. She told me all about it.

In **November**, the company officially closed. Both Bala and he were unemployed. Still, we had hope that we could find a way to survive. When he told Anu about his situation, she replied, "Didn't you once tell me we can't change the world? Why are you panicking now that you're the one facing problems? Are you expecting me to save you?"

That night, Aroon couldn't sleep. But by morning, Aroon had come up with a plan. He called Bala and Anu and asked her to bring Raj with her to a meeting. Everyone came, and he introduced them to each other.

He said, "Last night, I came up with a business idea. Please hear me out. The name of the plan is **Humanity Age**. It combines an old-age home and an orphanage. The idea is to transfer the knowledge and talent of the older generation to the younger generation. My brother Bala will provide the capital. Raj and the other elders will teach our children their talents and help them prepare for a special New Year's event. Anu will handle promotion and advertising. We'll hold a New Year 2020 celebration from 6 p.m. to 12 a.m. for just Rs. 10 per person in a large open space. I want the last 10 minutes of the event to speak to the crowd and share our vision."

He continued, "I'd like to hear your thoughts. First, my brother."

Bala said, "I may not believe in big dreams, but I believe in human talent. This is one chance I must help both the orphaned children and the elders. I'm in."

Then Raj spoke, "I never imagined that what we've lived through could inspire such a beautiful idea."

Aroon turned to Anu and said, "Thank you. You're the one who inspired me to think this way."

That night, Anu messaged him:

'You are the most amazing person I've ever met. I want to continue my life with you. I'll wait until New Year's. Give me your answer then.'

In **December**, they started working as fast as they could, and everything went smoothly. One day, Bala and Aroon discussed Anu's marriage proposal. Bala was excited for him and said, "That's great news!" But Aroon told him that I had a different wish.

Bala asked, "What is your wish?"

Aroon replied, "I don't want to get married. I want to dedicate my life to service—like A.P.J. Abdul Kalam, Swami Vivekananda, and Mother Teresa."

Bala nodded, then asked, "But you know, all the people you mentioned were born because their parents got married. If their parents hadn't married, they wouldn't have existed to do what they did. Marriage doesn't stop success. If you have a mission and a vision, nothing will stop you. And after marriage, your responsibilities may even push you to work harder."

He added, "This is just my view, based on my life experience. The decision is yours."

His words made him think differently.

On **December 31, 2019**, they were ready to showcase the talents of both the elderly and the children. Anu eagerly waited for my reply. But by 5:00 p.m., no one had arrived at the event. They started losing hope.

Aroon told everyone, "We're doing something good. God will help us. Don't give up."

By 5:40 p.m., people started arriving, family after family. They were filled with joy. By 6 p.m., the auditorium was full, and Anu began hosting the show. But Aroon wasn't there yet.

He went into John's old office and looked at his photo. He whispered, "You were right. The New Year does bring change. It turned me from a student into an entrepreneur."

After returning, behind of stage, Aroon sent Anu a message about marriage, but she was too busy on stage to see it.

Meanwhile, backstage, Bala asked Raj, "Can my wife and I adopt you as our father? We've also decided to adopt two children."

Raj burst into tears and replied, "Of course, my son."

At 11:50 p.m., Anu told the audience, "For the next 10 minutes, the lights will be turned off for a special New Year's moment." She walked offstage.

In the darkness, my voice echoed through the speakers. At that moment, Anu read my message:

"Hi Anu, I know you're eagerly waiting for my answer. I like you too. But we've only known each other for 11 months, and look how many changes we've already experienced. My wish is that we continue our friendship and business for one more year. If all goes well, then we'll get married. Don't lose hope—hope is everything in life."

Tears filled Anu's eyes.

On the mic, he continued, "Hi friends, I'm Aroon. I want to share something important. This event was planned just a month ago, but it has shown us the power of unity. The elders in our organisation are like gold—they have wisdom, skills, and kindness. I thank the children of these elders for placing them in old age homes, because it gave us this opportunity to learn from them. You didn't see their abilities—you only saw their age. But we've discovered their worth."

"Our children are like diamonds. They've managed both their studies and this event with brilliance. Together, we've proven that when humans join hands, nothing is impossible."

At **11:59 p.m.**, Anu typed:

"If you had said yes, I wouldn't have been this happy. I'm already happy seeing the changes in you and knowing we have hope for a better year ahead. Happy New Year."

At that moment, Aroon addressed the audience again:

"Now we want you to join hands with us and reach for the sky. We have 15 seconds left until the New Year. I'll end with one message: *Don't make New Year's resolutions—take New Year's action.* The countdown begins now."

10, 9, 8, 7, 6, 5, 4, 3, 2, 1...

The lights came back on.

He looked at my phone and saw Anu's message. he smiled and texted her:

"Happy New Year, Ma."

At that same moment, a voice rang out:

"Wish you and your family a Happy New Year 2020!"

THE END

Note to the reader:

Wishing you and your family a Happy New Year 2020. I hope this year brings a positive change in all our lives.

• • •

CHAPTER II

V. M. Krishna

A man named Varun (age 29) and a woman named Meenu (age 27) got married with the support of their parents, witnessed by a few people in a temple. Their parents gave them a child and said the child was lucky to witness his parents' wedding. The couple named the child V. M. Krishna. However, the people around them did not understand what was happening and began gossiping. So, the parents decided to explain everything.

They began telling the story of their children's past lives. Two years earlier, Varun (then 27) and Meenu (then 25) had an arranged marriage. Over time, they grew to truly love and care for each other, having never loved anyone before. When they were alone, they used affectionate nicknames like "da," "di," "pa," and "ma." They both worked hard at big companies during the week and spent quality time together on weekends—visiting each other's families, eating together, going out, and making many compromises for the sake of their relationship. Though they occasionally had playful fights and arguments, they celebrated birthdays and anniversaries joyfully.

Life was going smoothly, and one day, Meenu had good news—she was pregnant. Everyone was overjoyed. Varun took great care of Meenu, and she deeply loved him. They dreamed of their baby's arrival. After 10 months, they welcomed their child. At the hospital, Varun kissed Meenu's forehead and said they would have so much fun with their cute baby.

When it came time to choose a name, Meenu suggested they combine their initials for the baby's surname—Varun's first letter and Meenu's first letter. But Varun rejected the idea. He said society wouldn't accept it, and people would talk badly about them and their child. He insisted they use only his name for the surname.

This made Meenu angry. She said, "We both created this child. I carried our baby for 10 months. I want to feed our child, love our child, and yet I have no right to include my name? It's like I'm the mechanic and you're the owner. I go through the process and pain, and you get the credit?"

Her words angered Varun. He told her to stop. "I treat you as my equal," he said, "but I'm afraid of what society will say."

Meenu wasn't convinced. "I don't care about society. I want my rights."

Varun warned her, "Stop, or this will end in divorce." He left the room, went to the reception, filled out the birth certificate form, and registered the child's name as V. Krishna.

It broke Meenu's heart. But she was ready for it. A month later, they divorced.

After the separation, they lived with their respective parents. Both Varun and Meenu missed each other and their child deeply. Varun missed his wife and baby so much that he couldn't focus on his work. He became disturbed, and it affected his job. He finally shared his feelings with his parents.

"I miss my family," he confessed.

His parents asked, "What changed now?"

Varun replied, "When I was small, I also thought about keeping my mother's name as my surname. But I realised we can't change society."

His parents asked, "Do you know how divorce came into existence, like you, if the first couple in India were to file for divorce? Did they care what society would say? Today, we don't know what divorce means, and people will not get divorced when they aren't happy. It changed society's thinking. So why can't you change this, too? Initially, people will talk, but with time, they will understand."

Meanwhile, Meenu told her parents she wanted to reunite with Varun, but she still wanted her rights also.

Her parents scolded her. "We're not against your rights," they said, "we're questioning your actions. Your ego caused this."

Meenu asked, "What do you mean by ego?"

Her parents replied, **Ego means 'Everything Goes Out.'** When you divorced Varun, your happiness, your memories, the fun and fights, the life you shared—all of it was left with him, now that you couldn't share it. You had every right to fight for your name, but why did you accept divorce?"

She couldn't answer.

Both sets of parents answered their children, "What can we do to bring you back together?" They smiled and advised them to remarry each other. "No law can break a true relationship. Laws are made by people, for people. If there's a legal issue, we'll support you—even if it means fighting to change the law."

Varun and Meenu were overjoyed. Varun called Meenu and asked to meet her and their child the next evening in the park.

The next morning, Varun went to the government office and applied to change his name, adding his mother's name to his surname, and did the same for his child.

That evening, they met in the park. For five minutes, neither of them spoke. When Varun saw his child's face, tears filled his eyes.

He began, "I missed you both so much. I can't live without you."

He showed her the name-change form: **V. M. KRISHNA.**

"We need to set a good example for future generations," he said. "Let's remarry on the same date as our original wedding day, next week."

Meenu kissed him on the cheek and said, "I love you so much. I'm sorry for divorcing you; instead, I & our child want to torture you," which made them laugh.

Varun shared what his parents told him, and Meenu said her parents had said the same.

"I love both of you," Varun said, smiling at Meenu and their baby.

Their parents arranged the remarriage.

After finishing the story of their children's past, one of the witnesses—a lawyer—said, "According to the law, there is no issue with remarriage to the same person. If all children had parents like this, and all parents had children like this, there would be no divorce cases in court."

THE END

• • •

CHAPTER III

Achievement

Three boys, Adi, Bala, and Raj, were studying in the 12th grade at the same school. They had been close friends since 11th grade. They often shared what happened at school with their parents. However, Raj's parents did not talk to him daily as he was in an isolated hostel while his parents lived in the UAE.

As they prepared for their board exams, they studied diligently. When the results were announced, Adi secured the highest marks in the school with 90%, Bala scored 85%, and Raj achieved 80%. The school organised a special meeting to honour students who scored more than 75% in their 12th-grade exams. An email was sent out, inviting all students and their parents to attend the event.

On the day of the meeting, all the students arrived before their parents. Adi came on his bike. His father, Santhosh, and his mother, Kavitha, took seats in the front row. Other parents started arriving. Raj's mother, Sri, attended the event alone as his father was unable to come due to some business commitments. She sat next to Santhosh but did not notice him for a while. Bala's father, Muthu, a famous music director, and his mother, Divya, arrived late and sat in the last row.

The program began, and the students were honoured from the lowest to the highest scores. At that moment, Sri and Santhosh noticed each other and were shocked. Sri asked Santhosh, "What have you achieved in life? Your photos never appeared on TV or in newspapers. You once told me you would achieve something great, but now you're just sitting here. I am sure someone will help you get here." Santhosh did not respond; he simply smiled.

At that moment, the school principal called Adi onto the stage to receive his award. Adi invited his father to join him. To everyone's surprise, Santhosh confidently walked up to the stage. Sri was left speechless.

When Santhosh took the microphone, the audience applauded. He thanked them and asked why they were clapping. The crowd responded, "Adi has achieved success, but their children haven't reached that level."

Santhosh then said, "We all can achieve something every day in life. Even I, too, have achieved many things, like giving birth to Adi."

The audience was confused and asked what he meant. Santhosh began sharing his past. He explained that during his college days, he was just an ordinary student. His uncle's daughter, Kavitha, had suffered facial injuries in an accident during her childhood, which left her with scars. She liked Santhosh and confessed her feelings to him, but he treated her as a friend. At the time, he was interested in a junior girl in college, Sri, but he never mentioned her name to Kavitha.

Santhosh planned to propose to Sri on their farewell day. However, two days before the event, he and his friends went trekking on a mountain. Unfortunately, he slipped and fell between two cliffs. Miraculously, he survived, but his legs were severely injured, and he couldn't walk. Doctors told him he might recover, but that it would take years. When Sri came to visit him, he confessed his feelings for her. However, she rejected him, saying, "How can I live with you if we cannot enjoy life like other couples?" Her words shattered him, and he vowed to prove his worth.

For the next three years, he couldn't achieve much and worked in his father's business from home. His parents eventually pressured him to marry Kavitha. After the wedding, he confessed to Kavitha that he had initially liked someone else and offered her a divorce if she was unhappy. Kavitha responded, "Even when you told me you didn't like me, I never changed my mind because true love is one-sided." With the support of his mother and wife, he underwent extensive treatment and eventually regained his ability to walk after five years. He then built a happy life with his family. The audience clapped in admiration.

Santhosh then asked, "What is achievement? What does it mean? Who are the real achievers?" A parent stood up and said, "Achievers are people like Dr. A.P.J. Abdul Kalam and M.S. Dhoni."

Santhosh smiled and replied, "First, let's understand the meaning of 'achievement.' The full form of ACHIEVEMENT is **A - Attitude & Aim C - Concentration H - Hard work I - Interest E - Experience V - Value E - Encourage M - Mentor E - Enjoy N - Normal people T - Try**

We all achieve things daily. For example, when a child first learns to walk, they have a goal (**aim**). They develop an **attitude** to succeed and **concentrate**. They **work hard** by trying repeatedly to walk without falling because they are **interested** in walking like others. When parents see their child's efforts, they **encourage** them with kind words. These words hold **value**, and they bring **enjoyment** to the child. Through multiple attempts, they **mentor** themselves and gain **experience**. And, eventually, learn to walk in various situations (like how to walk at home, outside, with slippers, and without them). But at the end of the day, we are all just normal people who achieved it by **trying**.

Achievement isn't about being the first, a topper, or someone who does something unique. True achievement is about improving your own life. While not everyone may become like Abdul Kalam, some may surpass him."

Santhosh continued, "When my son scored 75% in 10th grade, we gifted him a phone. Now, since he got his license last week, we gifted him a new bike." A teacher asked, "Why did you give him a phone when he scored only 75%? Isn't it a bad habit to reward children like this? Won't he expect something for everything he does?"

Santhosh replied, "It is not a bad habit; it is encouragement. We all work with expectations. For example, we work for money.

Parents raise children, hoping they will care for them in old age. Even God expects us to do good deeds before granting us blessings. Rewards teach children responsibility. Our grandparents did the same when they gave us money on our birthdays and taught us to use it wisely." Another parent stood up and said, "I expect nothing from my children."

Santhosh responded, "That is a mistake. You should teach your children that it is their responsibility to care for you in your old age." And everyone clapped. Then, the teacher invited Adi's mother, Kavitha, to the stage, saying she was the backbone of Santhosh and Adi. Kavitha responded, "We are not each other's backbone. We are equals and stand beside each other."

She shared her story as well: "As a child, I was a cute girl who loved singing on stage and in temples. But one day, while riding my bicycle, my brakes failed, and I met with an accident that changed my life. My parents encouraged me to continue singing, but I only sang for my family. I also started writing short stories." Muthu, overwhelmed with guilt, started to cry. He stepped forward and confessed, "I was responsible for your accident."

Everyone was shocked. Muthu explained that 25 years ago, when they were in 7th grade, he had planned to cheat on his final exam, but Kavitha aunty had informed the teacher. Out of anger and peer pressure, he cut the brakes on her bicycle before leaving town. He never expected it to have such severe consequences. He had spent years searching for her to apologise.

Adi, furious, rushed to hit Muthu, but Bala tried to stop him, but Santhosh stopped him. Santhosh explained, "Muthu made a mistake, but he has now achieved something great—he admitted his fault publicly despite his status. That takes courage. "Muthu offered to help Kavitha restore her face, but Santhosh refused. "I love her for who she is, not how she looks," he said. Divya, Muthu's wife, then invited Kavitha to sing in Muthu's next film, and she happily accepted.

Sri also apologised and suggested that their children remain friends. Santhosh replied, "That is up to them, but we can all become family friends." Everyone left the event feeling happy and inspired.

THE END

• • •

CHAPTER IV

God's Plan & Human Actions

"GOD stands for Great Organism, which Determines our actions.

Vijay was born into a middle-class family. His best friend, Bala, came from a similar background. They were classmates and had been close friends since childhood. As they both belonged to middle-class families, their parents constantly encouraged them to study hard and to secure good jobs. Vijay was a diligent student from a young age, while Bala was an average student. However, both excelled in sports and possessed good character.

When they reached the 9th grade, their education became more challenging as they transitioned to the CBSE curriculum. They sought advice from their parents on how to study effectively. Their parents advised them to be realistic, write what they understood, share their thoughts on the topic, and answer based on their interpretation, as all questions were related to real life.

Bala followed this advice and prepared well for the board exams, but Vijay assumed it would be easy and focused solely on memorising answers from the textbook. In the 10th-grade board exams, most questions were directly from the book, except for a few in the science paper that required application-based answers. Bala managed to write responses based on his understanding, but Vijay struggled to answer those questions. As a result, Bala scored higher overall, while Vijay performed well but lagged behind Bala in science. Vijay questioned his parents, saying, "I studied the entire book, yet I didn't score well in science. Why?" His parents explained, "Exams are not about copying from textbooks like xerox machines. In real life, we need people who can think, create, and innovate."

After the 10th grade, Bala chose the science stream, while Vijay opted for commerce. As they were now in different streams, they made new friends. Bala was social, and he interacted with everyone in his class, whereas Vijay was focused on his studies. However, he gradually learned how to answer unfamiliar questions and managed his time wisely.

One of Vijay's classmates, Lakshmi, became a good friend to him. They discussed education and life together, and Vijay developed a crush on her. However, he remembered the promise he made to his parents—that they would arrange his marriage at the right time. Though he never expressed his feelings, he hoped to marry someone like her.

Vijay spent most of his time studying, watching TV for two hours daily, and chatting on WhatsApp for an hour. While studying, he often reflected on his past and future. Bala, on the other hand, explored his other talents and was less focused on academics. Lakshmi was an average student, and her parents did not pressure her to excel. Eventually, Vijay scored excellent marks, Bala performed moderately well, and Lakshmi remained an average student.

After completing school, they all joined different colleges. Vijay and Lakshmi had lost touch, while Bala struggled to get into a reputed college. In college, Bala fell in love with Priya, a classmate from a wealthy family. However, he developed a bad habit of gambling, which Priya and his parents disapproved of.

They urged him to stop. After completing their degrees, Priya's parents accepted their love, but Bala's parents did not. Nevertheless, Priya and Bala got married with her family's support, and Bala joined his father-in-law's business.

Meanwhile, Vijay secured a good job, and his parents arranged a marriage for him. When he went to meet his prospective bride, he was shocked to see that it was Lakshmi. He immediately announced that he had known her from school and had once had a crush on her. With everyone's approval, they got married.

For two years, life was smooth. Bala became the managing director of his business, while Vijay and Lakshmi continued to earn well. However, Bala started donating 10% of the business profits to the poor and orphanages without informing his in-laws. When an audit was conducted, Priya's father questioned the reduced profit margin.

The auditor revealed that Bala had been allocating a portion of the profits without providing proper statements. Priya suspected that Bala was still gambling, and her father speculated that he might be secretly giving money to his parents.

When Bala came home, Priya confronted him about gambling. In frustration, he raised his hand against her.

Outraged, Priya's parents asked him to leave their house and business. Bala, unable to return to his parents' home, wandered the streets. While walking, he was hit by a car, driven by none other than Vijay. Recognising his friend, Vijay rushed him to the hospital.

After an hour, Bala regained consciousness. Vijay asked him what had happened, and Bala narrated his ordeal. He lamented, "Why is God doing this to me?" Vijay responded, "God has the same plan for everyone, but our actions alter His course."

Bala, confused, asked for an explanation. Vijay elaborated, "**GOD stands for Great Organism, which Determined** our actions in this world, which determines our future based on our past and present actions."

Vijay gave several examples:

During our board exams, our parents advised us to write our thoughts. You followed their advice and scored well, but I didn't. The situation was reversed in the 12th grade when I adapted and improved."

"Like you, I had feelings for Lakshmi, but I respected my parent's wishes and didn't express them. As a result, God planned for me to marry her."

"You had a bad habit of gambling and lost money. Now, you donated to charity but failed to communicate with Priya. Because of this, she misunderstood you."

"You left your parents behind, and now Priya has left you. God is making you experience what it feels like to be abandoned."

"You got into an accident, and it was my car that hit you. This, too, is a part of God's plan to save you. Perhaps your good deed—donating to the poor—prevented something worse from happening."

Meanwhile, at Priya's home, they received a message about a missing check. Upon calling the bank, they discovered that Bala had signed the check for a charitable donation, which accounted for the missing business profits.

Realising their mistake, Priya and her parents called Bala, but Vijay answered and explained everything. They immediately rushed to the hospital.

Before they arrived, Vijay advised Bala, "Before making any decision, think carefully. God observes our present actions and plans accordingly for our future. Life is like an exam—if you prepare well and write the right answers, your future will be easier. If you don't, life will become more difficult. Our partners, friends, teachers, and real-life situations teach us both good and bad lessons. Think before you act."

When Priya arrived, she apologised for her misunderstanding. She and Bala decided to reunite with their parents.

They apologised for their past mistakes and expressed their desire to live together. Bala's parents forgave them, and they all lived together happily.

THE END

• • •

CHAPTER V

LAWS

**L - Legal, A - Actions on, W - Wrong, S - Surroundings/
Society.**

The new Youth Chief Minister (CM) of Tamil Nadu, Tarun, was announced at a public meeting the day after he assumed office. The event was attended by the press and the public and was broadcast live on television. As Tarun began his speech, he stated that he would not be a typical CM like others before him but would instead be as strict as Hitler for every person in Tamil Nadu. His statement left everyone confused. However, he continued, asking the public first to understand his reason.

He said, "Many of you may know little about me, but today I will tell you everything. I am just 27 years old and came from a middle-class family. I studied diligently during my school days, but I have never watched the news on TV or read newspapers. My parents often scolded me and urged me to stay informed about the world. So, I began reading the newspaper for 30 minutes every day, and I was shocked by what I discovered. I found that 25% of the news was good, while 75% was bad."

He continued, "Observing my surroundings, I noticed the prevalence of negative incidents, which disturbed me deeply. I discussed this with my parents, asking why such things happen in the world. They told me, 'We are ordinary people; we cannot change anything. Just ignore it and focus on your own life.' But I couldn't ignore it. I argued with them, believing that these bad things would eventually affect everyone, directly or indirectly. My parents then told me that if I truly wanted to bring change, I needed the power of knowledge. So, I focused on my studies and thought about this issue every day."

"I pursued a law degree (B.L.) and excelled in my studies, secured the top rank in my college and earned a gold medal. I was then granted to do a two-year course in the world's best law college in the USA. While studying there, I made some close friends. Deepak, whose parents were originally from India but had settled in the USA as citizens. I learned about various international laws. Over time, Deepak and I fell in love."

"One day, I shared my plans with all my friends. I told them that I wanted to return to Tamil Nadu, to stand in the election contest for CM and to implement new laws. They all supported my dreams."

"After our final exams, I visited Deepak's parents to discuss our relationship. They accepted our love but placed one condition: I had to stay in the USA and obtain U.S. citizenship. For that, I refused. Deepak tried to persuade me, but I told her I could not abandon my dreams and my parents for her. She made every effort to convince her parents, but they did not agree."

"After returning to Tamil Nadu, a few friends who also shared my vision joined me, along with some of my old friends. Together, we established a new political party last year. We engaged college students, sharing our party's vision and plans. Due to the unstable government, people believed in us and voted for us. That is how I became the CM of Tamil Nadu."

He then continued, "Now, I am going to introduce 10 important laws."

One of the public members asked, "Does the state government have the power to change national laws? Isn't there a long process involved?"

The CM Tarun replied, "Yes, you are right, brother. However, the state government does have some power to modify and introduce laws that benefit the state and improve people's lifestyles, by global legal standards. We have been working on these changes for the past six months. Yesterday, after the office, we discussed these laws with the Governor and the Prime Minister. Fortunately, this morning, we received approval to introduce and modify certain laws.

First, let me explain the full form of **LAWS: L - Legal, A - Actions on, W - Wrong, S - Surroundings/Society.** I will now present the 10 basic laws aimed at addressing fundamental issues in our state. I know that some of you may not accept these laws, but I do not care about opposition."

<u>The 10 Laws:</u>

1) If a person steals out of desperation for survival, they will be imprisoned for 10 years. After serving their sentence, they will be given a government job. However, if they commit the same crime again, they will be imprisoned for life.

2) If a person commits rape, they will not be given the death penalty. Instead, the police will publicly punish them by permanently disabling the offending body part.

3) If a person commits murder, they will be executed immediately.

4) If parents report that their children have neglected them after inheriting property, the government will revoke the children's educational degrees, terminate their jobs, or seize their businesses immediately and the property which are inherited from them.

5) All alcohol shops and bars in Tamil Nadu will be permanently shut down.

6) If anyone wears torn clothing as a fashion statement in public, a nearby designated office will provide them with traditional tribal attire and take a photo of them. If a company in Tamil Nadu manufactures such clothes, it will be shut down. If these clothes are imported, their trade licenses will also be revoked.

7) If an unmarried couple is seen being too intimate in public, the police will take action and inform their parents. Love is a private matter and should not affect others in public spaces.

8) If a person defaults on repaying money, all their assets will be seized by the Income Tax Department. Additionally, all transactions above ₹500 must be conducted through banks only.

9) If a person is caught in an adulterous relationship, their partner has the right to kill them without facing punishment.

10) Any individual applying for foreign citizenship must pay ₹1 billion as a "foreign income tax" at the Indian embassy before they can acquire citizenship in another country.

After announcing the laws, the CM invited questions from the public. One young man asked, "Why should we pay ₹1 billion to become citizens of another country? How will you enforce this?"

The CM responded, "You receive an education here at a minimal cost, but then you leave for work and contribute to the development of another country. What happens to our nation then? We have Indian employees in every foreign embassy who maintain records of visa applications. Before processing your foreign citizenship, they will check if you have paid the ₹1 billion tax, which will be transferred to the Indian World Bank for national development."

A young woman asked, "Why should we not wear fashionable clothing? What difference does it make?"

The CM replied, "I understand your feelings, but let me ask you: Why wouldn't you wear traditional tribal clothing, which looks similar to modern torn fashion? If we marketed tribal attire as the latest trend, people would buy it from stores. We are not banning modern clothing entirely, but we want people to dress appropriately according to our cultural values. You should be mindful of how others perceive you in public. This law applies to both men (wearing torn jeans) and women (wearing torn dresses)."

A journalist asked, "What if the public does not comply with your laws? What actions will you take?"

The CM answered, "These laws are introduced to address key issues in the state. We believe that the people will support us because these are concerns that many ordinary citizens wanted to address but lacked the power to enforce. We are giving them the means to act. These laws will be in effect for the next five years. We hope for positive results.

"Finally, the CM thanked the public for listening and concluded, "I hope our state will become an example for others in India and around the world."

THE END

• • •

Friendship

One day, the teachers of KRMM School planned to celebrate Friendship Day. Every year, they would invite the 12th-grade students who had just graduated that year to do something special at the event so that future generations could understand the value of friendship.

When the Principal arrived, they had been discussing what had happened during the previous year's celebration. The students misbehaved after joining the college. They did inappropriate things on stage, but the teachers couldn't mention the negative incidents publicly. So, they only spoke positively, and the principal decided not to let it happen again.

However, one teacher, Sri Devi, wanted to invite her current students. She was confident that they would perform well because she had taught them for a year. She requested the principal to give them a chance based on her trust in them. The principal agreed with one condition and said, "I want something different this time—not just the usual friendship stories, plays, or talks."

Sri Devi's teacher replied, "Sure, ma'am. I know my students will do something new. Thank you, ma'am."

She called her students—Aroon, Aditya, Bharathi, and Hessa—and asked them to come to school the next day. When they arrived, she explained the principal's expectations. Later, the students met the principal.

The principal warned, "Do whatever you want, but if it is not beneficial for the students, I will insult you all on stage."

The students responded, "Okay, ma'am. We'll take care and do our best."

On Friendship Day, all the students gathered in the auditorium. The teachers and the Principal sat in the front row. Teacher Sri Devi introduced the performers, and the four students came to the stage, greeted everyone and sat down without holding any props.

Sri Devi teacher, announced, "My students, the stage is yours."

Aroon began, "Hi, my friends and teachers. What are we going to do today? We're going to have a conversation about friendship. I will tell a short story, and the others will talk about different types of friendship."

He started his story: "Imagine two friends—one is a ship captain and the other is the ship itself. One day, the captain sailed into the sea. When they had a conflict (they ran out of petrol), the ship refused to help and said, 'You didn't treat me well.' Then another ship approached and asked what had happened. The captain explained the situation. The new ship offered help (by providing petrol), and eventually, the captain's ship reached land."

Aroon then asked, "Who are the best friends in this story?" No one answered, so he explained, "The captain and his ship are the best of friends because even after their fight, they reconciled and remained together."

A student asked, "Is this story about relationships?" Aroon replied, "No, relationships are based on blood ties, while friendship doesn't consider age, gender, caste, or anything else. It's about how well we connect."

Bharathi took over. "Hello, friends. How many types of friendship do you know?" One student said, "Two friends and one best friend." Bharathi replied, "No," and pulled out a chart from her bag. It showed two circles and a dot inside the smallest circle.

She explained, "The big outer circle represents non-living friends who help us survive—like water, land, and eco-friendly machines like cars and bikes. Treat them as friends, too."

Aditya continued, "The second circle includes living friends—your family, friends, animals (like cows that give milk), and people from different occupations who help in daily life."

Hessa then said, "My friends mentioned the two big circles. But I'll talk about the full stop—the most important part."

She asked, "Who is your best friend?" Students gave answers like friends, parents, the world, or God. Hessa said, "I don't accept those answers. I'll divide friendship into two categories: visible and invisible best friends."

The audience was confused, so she continued, "God is powerful and guides us. But my other best friend knows everything about me—it's my soul."

Everyone laughed, thinking she was joking. She replied, "I'll prove it." She invited two best friends on stage, blindfolded one, and asked the other to guide him. He successfully reached his friend.

Then, she took away the guide and gave the blindfolded student a walking stick. He used it to detect the stage's edge and still managed to reach his friend.

She asked, "Who guided you?" He said, "The walking stick and my instincts." Hessa responded, "That's what I meant. You can tell 99.9% of your life to your best friend, but your soul knows everything. It speaks to you even when you're bored or struggling."

She continued, "In exams, if you don't know the answers, close your eyes, your inner voice may help. If everyone says you're wrong but your inner self says you're right, trust it. Your soul can even speak through dreams."

"So, your soul is your invisible best friend."

After Hessa's speech, the four friends said, "Thank you all. Happy Friendship Day!"

Everyone stood up and clapped. The principal came on stage and said, "I've never seen such a Friendship Day celebration. I've learned a lot. From now on, I'll celebrate this day every year. I don't worry about other's opinions, because my bestie—my soul—is telling me to do so."

She honoured the students and Sri Devi on stage.

THE END

• • •

CHAPTER VII

Hobbies

One Saturday morning, on 5th June 2023 at 9 A.M., a train started from Bangalore to Chennai. It would take seven hours to reach Chennai. Siva, a teenage boy, was seated in seat number 11, with the boys named Kumar and Ravi sitting beside him. On the opposite side, two girls named Priyanka and Durga were also seated. As the train began to move faster, Durga took her book and started to read. Ravi listened to music with his earphones, and Priyanka talked with someone on the phone.

After some time, Siva introduced himself to Kumar: "I'm Siva, and I'm studying BBA in Bangalore. Since the semester exam is over, I'm going home and looking to join a small business as an intern." Kumar replied, "I'm going to Chennai to participate in an under-19 hockey match that's happening tomorrow evening."

At that moment, they heard Priyanka was talking to her mother on the phone: "I got on the train, and I'll reach Chennai by 4 p.m. and be home by 5 p.m. But my phone battery is low, so I might not be able to call you."

After the call, she asked the one who was seated next to her, "Excuse me, sister, do you have a Type-C charger?" But Durga replied that she didn't.

Kumar offered, "You can use my power bank; it has a Type-C charger." Priyanka was pleased and thanked him..plugged her phone and joined the conversation by introducing herself. "I'm Priyanka. I completed a visa. Com degree and I'm going to Chennai for an RJ interview at a FM radio station on Tuesday morning." They continued talking about their families, friends, and favourite things.

Suddenly, Durga's book fell as she dozed off, waking her up. Priyanka picked it up and handed it back to her. Durga thanked her and introduced herself: "I'm Durga. I'm going to Chennai for my wedding, which is next week, on Sunday, June 13th. I'm the only child, so I feel shy talking to new people. So I read storybooks and try solving puzzles, which are my hobbies, but these days I fall asleep when I start reading."

Siva responded, "Thank you, sister, for giving us a new topic to discuss about hobbies! My hobbies are playing chess, listening to songs with meaningful lyrics, and talking to new people to learn new things and stay informed. What about you guys?"

Kumar smiled and said, "I don't have any specific hobbies—maybe playing hockey." Durga replied, "Bro, that's not a hobby! Since you're trained to play for India, it's your focus, and it's like more of a job or duty."

Priyanka added, "My hobbies include watching IPL matches—I love CSK and MSD—and I will watch every new movie when it's released. Because of that, my phone battery will always be low. Once it charges up to 50%, I'll be busy on my phone again, guys."

Siva laughed and asked, "Who told you these are hobbies? And you forgot to include eating, drinking, and sleeping!"

Priyanka snapped back, "Nowadays, everyone treats these things as hobbies. My dad watches Facebook videos about politics, my mom watches WhatsApp videos about COVID, cooking, Gods, and funny memes. My friends make reels and post on social media or go out on dates. What's wrong with that?"

Siva replied, "You're not wrong, but we're fooling ourselves and those around us."

"Why, bro?" Priyanka asked.

Siva explained, "Please hear me out. As you said, we all do these things. But we've forgotten the real meaning of hobbies. Hobbies are meaningful—they help us get something from society, give something back, or make us feel happy during our free time without wasting money or hurting others. They should help us relax mentally or physically when under pressure."

Durga chimed in, "He's right. I'm a psychology postgraduate. Hobbies can be classified into four types:

1. **Making ourselves happy or healthy** – playing a musical instrument, listening to music, doing yoga, drawing, singing, etc.
2. **Making others happy** – helping people, doing small kind acts, or offering free performances with your skills.

Kumar interrupted, "Sister, you're spot on! I used to remember everyone's birthdays and weddings and wish them on Facebook, but very few remembered mine. So, I stopped doing that a few years ago."

Siva said, "Just be yourself and do the right thing. We all get frustrated, but if we keep doing good, it'll come back to us one day."

Kumar replied, "Okay, bro. Let's see."

Priyanka then asked Durga to continue with the remaining two types of hobbies.

Durga said:

3. **Part-time earning hobbies** – writing stories, poetry, or selling creative work while having another main job.

4. **Time-pass hobbies** – just passing time with no real benefit to life.

Siva turned to Priyanka: "So what you said about your hobbies, and your parents and friends' habits, mostly fall into the fourth type. Maybe some of them are useful, like if you gain general knowledge for a quiz show. But scrolling through Instagram and casual dating are just time-pass activities. Still, everyone needs some fun to create good memories, like we are now. Just keep it in pleasure, and life will be more meaningful."

He added, "We're almost in Chennai—probably an hour away. Before we part, could you turn on your phone and see if there are any useful notifications or good news in the world?"

She turned it on but saw only one major news item—tragic news of a 3-train collision in Odisha that started at 9 a.m. and happened around 1 p.m., killing nearly 200 people. She was shocked and told everyone.

Siva said, "If you had seen this news earlier, you'd have been scared about our journey. But instead, we had a joyful time."

Priyanka replied, "You're right. But now I'm scared we'll all be separated in half an hour. Can we stay in touch?" Everyone nodded with sad expressions.

Ravi then showed them a message on his phone: "I'm Ravi Dum (I'm differently abled and cannot talk), so I wear headphones to avoid attention. I heard all your conversations and liked them. I studied IT and came to Bangalore for a government exam. My father owns a photo studio in Chennai, but due to my condition and modern selfie culture, the business has declined. In my free time, I enjoy taking nature photos and editing videos. I wish I could talk to you all, but this is my reality. Let's create a WhatsApp group to stay in touch."

Everyone loved Ravi's idea. Siva said, "We already have too many unnecessary groups—let's make this one useful." They agreed and created a group called **"Hobbies Mate."**

When they reached Chennai, Priyanka forgot to return the power bank. Her mother asked what she ate for lunch, and Priyanka replied, "The conversation was so interesting, I didn't feel hungry."

That night, Kumar messaged the group: "Guys, tomorrow is Sunday. I hope you're free—please come to the stadium and support me." Everyone replied, "Sure, bro." The next day, they met, encouraged Kumar. He introduced his friends to his coach. Priyanka thoughtfully brought the power bank and returned.

On Tuesday, they all wished Priyanka good luck. During her interview, the interviewer asked, "Why did you write 'talking to new friends' as a hobby on your resume?" She shared the train story and got selected.

Afterwards, she messaged, "Thanks, Siva bro and Durga's sister. I got the job by sharing what we discussed on the train!"

On Wednesday, Siva visited Ravi's studio and met his father. He asked, "Can I do my internship here as a cashier for six months?" and joined the business.

On Thursday, Durga invited everyone to her wedding on Sunday. Everyone except Ravi said, "Sure, sister." Ravi replied privately, "Sorry, I can't come. People will notice my condition. Wishing you a happy married life."

Durga visited Ravi's studio with her fiancé and booked wedding photography. She told Ravi, "Now it's your job to make us look like a hero and heroine in our album!" Everyone smiled. "Don't be afraid of what others think—it's your chance to shine."

On Friday night, Kumar felt lonely and went to sleep. At 11:55 p.m., someone knocked. When he opened, it was his train friends, hockey teammates, and coaches with a birthday cake! Shocked, he asked them, "How did you all know?"

Siva said, "Ravi, bro noticed your seat and jersey number were both 12. He used his IT skills to find your old account and learned it's your birthday." Kumar became so overwhelmed and thanked them. With Ravi's help, he recovered his old account and resumed wishing others.

On Sunday, everyone attended Durga's wedding. Ravi took beautiful photos and edited the videos with wedding songs. He shared the soft copy that night in the group and said, "The photo album will be ready in 3 days. Consider this video as my gift."

Everyone loved the video. Priyanka gave Ravi a free ad on the radio, Kumar spoke to his coach about broadcasting hockey matches on TV with Ravi's help, and Durga sent her wedding video to friends. This brought Ravi's business to grow. He and Siva became business partners.

Inspired, Siva proposed turning the group into a **public platform for promoting creative hobbies** with all 5 members as admins. Everyone agreed to it. Now, helping others has become their new hobby.

THE END

• • •

CHAPTER VIII

Happy Student's Day

Imagine – This story is happening in the year 2070.

Abi, a girl studying in the 9ᵗʰ grade in Chennai, belonged to a rich family that had been wealthy for more than five generations. She lived in a joint family with her parents and grandparents, Sam and Kavi. Her parents were working professionals, so after school, Abi would come home, complete her homework, and spend time with her grandparents until her parents returned.

Her grandfather, Sam, was a Chartered Accountant (CA) and an ACCA, while her grandmother, Kavi, had worked at ISRO until her retirement.

On **October 14,** after school, Abi came home. Kavi asked how to switch on the AC using a smartphone, and Abi showed her. Abi told her grandmother she didn't have any homework that day and that she wouldn't be going to school the next day because of the Student's Day celebration. Kavi asked why she didn't like Student's Day. Abi replied, "I feel bad being born a student because all I do is study." She then went to freshen up and returned to the dining table to have snacks with her grandparents.

At that moment, her grandfather said, "Being a student is a gift. Can I tell you about my student life since you don't have homework today?" Abi replied, "Yes!"

Sam began, "Let me start from 9th grade since that's where I remember the most. On the first day of school, just like you, I thought studying was boring. But my English teacher changed that. She asked us how we studied and understood lessons. We said we just memorised, read, and tried to understand. Then she introduced a new method. She asked questions about myself—my name, birthday, where I lived, my parents' names, how many years I'd studied at that school, and why I was there. I answered everything. She then said, 'See, I just learned everything about you. Education is like that—a game of questions and answers. So, never hesitate to ask questions.'

She then asked why schools have timetables. No one answered. She explained, 'It's to train you to balance things in life—happiness, sorrow, fun, boredom—along with building your talents.'

After that class, we all became close friends. My best friend was Ram. We even played cricket in class using paper balls and notebooks as bats. I would ask questions like: 'Where do we use definitions and integration in real life?' The teacher didn't know at first, but the next day she told us that these concepts are used by scientists and pilots to calculate distances. Ram once asked,

'Why are we studying history when it's all in the past?' The teacher explained that studying past mistakes, like those that caused the world wars, helps us avoid repeating them.

I once asked my science teacher, 'What is sex?' She calmly explained, 'Sex has two meanings. One is whether you're a boy or a girl. The other is a biological interaction between married couples to give birth to good students like you. That's enough for you to know for now.'

We had lots of small and big fights among friends. Sometimes we didn't talk, but we always helped each other when needed. We had nicknames for teachers—friendly ones—and even they knew but didn't mind as long as we stayed respectful. We also knew about bad words and things in the world, but we never did anything wrong. Knowing what's bad is also a kind of knowledge.

In 10th grade, I worked very hard. No TV, outings, or movies—just studying for board exams. After the exams, I felt like a monkey set free in the jungle! I had a great time with friends and family. But an hour before the results came, my heartbeat sped up even though I was confident. When I saw my excellent marks, I felt like eating ice cream on a hot day! Everyone praised me.

12th grade was similar, but better, because of our farewell day. Boys wore suits, girls wore sarees, we took photos, had small crushes, and shared food. The teachers were friendly, and by the end of the day, we felt sad about leaving our friends. The 12th exams came and went like the 10th.

Then, Kavi added, "In college, I learned that every subject is interlinked and with everything."

Abi didn't understand and asked for an example. Kavi asked her to fetch a glass of water. When Abi returned, she explained with water as an example:

- In different languages, water has different names (language subject).
- In biology, it's essential for all living beings.
- In chemistry, it's H_2O.

- In physics, it conducts electricity.
- In math, we measure its quantity.
- In history, it's part of many historical events.
- In geography, we study rainfall and rivers.
- In economics, water is a scarce resource.
- In accounts, scarcity affects pricing.
- In statistics, we study groundwater levels.
- In law, there was a legal battle over the Kaveri River.
- In computers, water bills are now digitised.

"This shows how people in different fields view the same thing differently."

Sam continued: "The night before my first college day, I couldn't sleep from excitement, fear, and happiness. I asked my parents if it was okay. They said everyone goes through this. If you miss a night's sleep, it won't hurt. Just keep dreaming."

Ram and I joined the same college for B.Com. Like school, we made good friends. Sometimes we skipped class to have fun. As students, it was okay, but once you start working, skipping work affects your salary and lifestyle.

There were many lovebirds in our college, claiming 'true love,' but most of it was nonsense. Ram once asked why I wasn't in love. I said I believed in two types of love:

1. **True love** – loving from the heart, not just physical touch.
2. **One-sided love** – still pure and respectful.

Ram said, "Love is part of student life, too." I agreed and said, "That's why I love my parents." But deep down, I also wished to fall in love.

Life moved fast. I completed B.Com, MBA, and passed the CA Intermediate. My parents arranged for me to meet a girl, your grandma, Kavi. We met at a temple and talked about our likes and dislikes. We were very different, but we had similar views about love and respected each other. We agreed to get married after six months, since I was preparing for the CA Final and she had three months left to complete her PG in Rocket Science.

We spent those six months loving each other, like other couples, but with limits. We just held hands. We believed anything could happen anytime, so we respected boundaries.

One week before my exam, our parents fixed the wedding date—12 days after the exam. Kavi called me, but I am in class. I ignored it twice, but she kept calling. My teacher caught me and scolded me. Frustrated, I scolded Kavi afterwards, telling her not to disturb me for a week. Later, I found out why she called and felt bad. I apologised, but didn't get a reply. So I focus on my studies, but sometimes I get fear that our relationship will end.

On exam day, she texted: "All the best, mad." That one message convinced me she truly loved me. I thanked her, did well in the exam, and we got married.

Ram joked, "So it's a love marriage!" I laughed, "No, it's an arranged comes love marriage."

Since our family was wealthy, I pursued ACCA, and Kavi completed her doctorate in Rocket Science. I studied until age 35, and Kavi until 30. During this time, our son—your father—was born. Our parents raised him while we studied. Later, I took over the family business, and Kavi joined ISRO.

After hearing the whole story, Abi said, "You both are great studying till your 30s!"

Kavi smiled and said, "I also learned something from you today."

Abi asked, "What?"

Kavi replied, "You taught me how to turn on the AC with a smartphone! My Guru once told me—**Education is learning from our surroundings.**"

Then Sam asked, "Do you know why we celebrate Student's Day?"

Abi said, "No."

He explained, "Kavi's Guru was a brilliant student for 50 years and a great teacher until his last breath. He lived without hate, spreading knowledge and peace. The **UNO declared his birthday,**

October 15ᵗʰ as World Students Day. He is none other than Dr. A.P.J. Abdul Kalam."

Just then, Abi's parents came home. Abi told them, "I'm going to school tomorrow to celebrate Student's Day. I don't want to miss this wonderful gift of being a student!"

Her parents were very happy.

THE END

Note to the reader:

Wishing you a Happy Student's Day! Enjoy your life to the fullest.

• • •

CHAPTER IX

LIFES (3 parts)

A man and a woman stood in front of the court. The press approached them and asked if they were getting a divorce. As they thought about their past, memories flooded back. Their parents had been good friends because they belonged to the same caste, and as a result, their children, Jai (a boy) and Swetha (a girl), were close friends from childhood. They attended the same school and made two more friends, Surya and Divya.

Their friendship was filled with playing, fighting, helping, and discussing everything in life as they grew. When they reached their teenage years, their parents educated them about sex, the caste system, and other important aspects of life. However, Jai and Swetha did not believe in the caste system; they believed in true love. Among their group, all except Surya scored high marks.

However, Surya had a talent for marketing anything. Over time, they all moved to different parts of the country for their studies, but Jai and Swetha stayed in touch via WhatsApp daily.

Jai fell in love with a classmate, Viji, who was very beautiful, and Swetha fell for a stylish boy named Kathi. They often chatted about their love lives, but after six months, Swetha discovered that Kathi had tried to kiss her, and Jai found out that Viji had many past relationships she never mentioned. Heartbroken, they both ended their relationship and decided to listen to their parents.

They supported each other through their breakups, sharing many common thoughts and a few differences. Jai advised Swetha not to wear overly modern clothes and to use minimal makeup, as she was naturally beautiful. Swetha, in turn, advised Jai to drive carefully and always wear a helmet due to the rising number of accidents. However, they both ignored each other's advice.

As they focused on their studies, they texted less frequently but missed each other deeply. Their old memories made them realise they had developed feelings for each other, and eventually, they confessed their love. They started following each other's advice—Jai always wore a helmet, and Swetha dressed well but modestly. However, their increased chatting affected their grades, leading them to decide to limit their conversations.

After finishing their degrees, they revealed their love to their parents, who were surprised and asked them three questions:

1. "You are best friends, so you love each other. Do you understand the value of friendship?"
2. "What if we do not accept your relationship?"
3. "What are your plans after marriage?"

Jai answered, "We understand the value of friendship. We have two other best friends, but our love is based on major common thoughts, the same caste, and a deep friendship. I am not saying all friendships end in love, but true love often starts with friendship."

Swetha responded, "If you don't accept our love, we will wait for your approval throughout our lives because we love them deeply too."

However, they had no concrete plans for their future. Their parents advised them to pursue their postgraduate degrees and secure jobs first. They followed their parents' advice, with Jai completing a degree in production and Swetha qualifying as a CA. After completing their studies and securing stable jobs, their parents approved their marriage.

At their wedding, they invited Divya and Surya. Divya arrived with her wealthy husband, but Surya was absent. Later, they learned that Surya's behaviour had changed due to his lack of good academic results. Unable to secure a job, he worked as a labourer and had fallen into bad habits like drinking and smoking.

Jai advised him, "You work hard to earn money, but you waste it on habits that harm your health." Surya listened, and together, they discussed starting a new production business. With Divya providing the funds, Surya marketing manager, Swetha handling accounts & internal auditor and Jai overseeing production, they built a successful enterprise. Their teamwork strengthened the business, helping each other overcome weaknesses and become famous.

However, personal issues between Jai and Swetha led them to court. When the press asked about their divorce, they responded, "Living together and divorce are similar. Living together means being in a relationship as long as we like and leaving when we don't. The difference is that divorce is legal while living together is not. We have been friends since childhood and have fought many times—it's not a big deal. We are here for a business dispute, not a marital one."

Eventually, they had adorable twin babies. At their first birthday party, they took a group photo, symbolising the continuation of their journey.

•••

PART 2- EDUCATION AND CHARACTERS

Jai and Swetha had twins named Jayram (son) and Annapoorani (daughter), and they all lived with their grandparents in the same house. Their business and family life were going well. Since the twins were born, Swetha stopped going to the office regularly, but she worked from home and visited the office for two hours once a month while her grandparents took care of the children.

As they grew up with their grandparents, they listened to many small stories and had fun going to parks, playing games, watching movies, and watching YouTube cartoons. They also studied a little. When they turned ten and entered the 5th standard, they did well in their first-term exams. One weekend, they planned to go to a movie and eat out, but they received a message from the school about a Parent-Teacher Meeting (PTM) on the same day. Annapoorani became sad, fearing she would get low marks, and she didn't want to go out on the result day.

However, the family convinced her, deciding to visit the school first and then go out. When they met the teacher, she told them that Jayram had scored above 75 in all subjects, whereas Annapoorani had scored around 50. The teacher said this happened because Swetha hadn't checked whether her daughter had studied properly. Swetha assured the teacher that they would take care of her studies in the future. After the PTM, the family went to a movie and a hotel for dinner.

After eating, they got into the car, but Annapoorani suddenly broke down in tears over her low marks. Jayram asked everyone not to talk about it and told her to stop crying over small things. This made her angry, and she refused to talk to anyone. The next day, Jai tried to speak to Annapoorani, but she wasn't ready to listen. She said, "Jayram is more important than I, and you don't care about me." After hearing this, Jai called Jayram and explained to them both, "You are equally important to us. We did not discuss your marks yesterday because we wanted to enjoy our time together. But now, let's discuss it. How did you study?"

Jayram replied, "I memorised all the questions and answers, but Annapoorani said I just learned the concepts and keywords."

Jai asked them to recall a question from the test. They said, "What are the common things between plants and animals?" Jayram answered, "Both breathe and eat food to live." Annapoorani added, "All living organisms breathe and eat food, including plants and animals."

Jai then asked, "How many marks did you get for this question?" Jayram said, "I got 5 out of 5," while Annapoorani said, "I got 4.5 out of 5." Jai laughed, confusing them. They asked, "Why are you laughing? Are you mad?"

Jai replied, "Jayram did hard work, but Annapoorani did smart work." Jayaram didn't understand and got angry. Jai then asked them to hold their breath for five minutes. Within two minutes, they couldn't do it and breathed out. Jai turned to Jayram and asked, "Why couldn't you control your breath for five minutes?" Jayram replied, "Because I'm a living organism."

Jai smiled and said, "Now, you just proved what your sister wrote on paper. That is called smart work."

Annapoorani then asked, "Is smart work better than hard work in life? And why did my teacher say I got low marks?"

Jai explained, "Both are important. If you only work smart but don't focus on details, it will be a big mess. Hard work and smart work should be balanced, 50% of both is ideal. Also, no one is responsible for others' words and actions. When the teacher scolded us, we didn't get angry or upset. That's why your grandparents advise you to study both ways, ask questions, and find the correct answers. Never believe something without understanding it."

Hearing this, Annapoorani felt normal again. Life moved on. After the exams, Sports Day arrived. Jayam participated in a 200-meter race and secured second place. However, he was unhappy and told his family he felt ashamed for not coming first. Grandpa reassured him, "You tried your best and came second—be happy about it. First, love yourself and appreciate your efforts. Keep trying, and one day, you will win. Remember, winning and losing are like tossing a coin; they depend on three things—your hard work, timing, and fairness. Sometimes you win & sometimes you will lose, it's ok, try to learn new things."

To cheer them up, Grandpa took them to the mall. While buying gifts for Jayram, Annapoorani overheard some boys saying that boys are better than girls. She asked Grandpa, "What is the difference between boys and girls?"

Grandma replied, "We have both the sun and the moon, summer and winter, and 24 hours a day. They all have unique features, advantages, and disadvantages. For example, in summer, we can wear light clothes, but in winter, we need warm clothes. Likewise, boys and girls have their specialities. This world accepts both summer and winter equally, dividing them into six months each. AM and PM each have 12 hours. So why can't people accept that boys and girls are equal? Each person has their strengths and weaknesses, but we can overcome disadvantages by helping each other."

During a holiday, the family planned a three-day trip to Delhi. When packing, Jayram suggested bringing raincoats, but they dismissed the idea, saying there would be no rain in Delhi. They arrived in the afternoon and met their tour guide, Ram, who didn't appear friendly at first, making them uncomfortable. However, they had no choice but to go with him. On the first day, they refreshed themselves, had lunch, and visited the Red Fort and India Gate, where Ram explained their history.

That evening, they stopped for tea, but Ram didn't eat anything. The next day, they travelled to the Taj Mahal. Normally, the journey takes three hours from Delhi, but Ram drove slowly, taking four to five hours. When Jai asked why, Ram explained, I drove carefully because you have children and elderly family members."

While talking to Ram, Grandpa was surprised that he could discuss economic problems and solutions, even though he didn't know technical terms.

At breakfast the next day, Jayram wasted some food. Ram noticed this and later advised him, "If you can't finish your food, pack it up and eat it later. Many people don't have food in this world."

On the third day, while driving to the temple, Annapoorani asked her mother, "What is character?" Swetha replied, "Our appearance is God's creation, but our character is something we design ourselves."

Grandma asked Ram about his life. He revealed that he had lost his parents ten years ago, couldn't afford school, and worked as a labourer earning 20 rupees per day—just enough for two meals. Over time, he did various small jobs and learned about everything in Delhi.

When they reached the temple, it suddenly started raining. Jayram wore his raincoat, while others got drenched. They realised they should have listened to him.

While returning, Jayram asked his grandparents, "What is God to you?" They replied, "God is a powerful force that helps us in difficult times if we do good deeds."

As they ran towards the car, a fast-moving lorry approached. Ram saw it and saved both children. They thanked him deeply. At the airport, the kids realised Ram was a kind person, and they admired his wisdom.

Ram later told Annapoorani, "You asked about the character. In my opinion, God created everyone equally, but people have both good and bad characteristics. If your actions and words don't harm others, that is a good character."

Touched by this, Swetha asked Annapoorani to give an example of good and bad character. She replied, "Ram's uncle is a good character, and the policeman who took bribes for no reason is a bad character."

Jayram smiled, feeling that Ram was like a guardian angel who had saved them.

• • •

3rd part- Changes

They returned home for the weekend, took a rest, and started preparing for work. Since the children had grown up, Swetha resumed working at the office, while Jai helped with their homework. Their business began experiencing losses, so they worked hard while their children focused on their studies. They discovered that they were losing to a competitor company and decided to meet with them. To their shock, the owners were Kathi and Viji, their ex-lovers, who had married after college.

The four of them shared their past love stories. Jai and Swetha asked how Kathi and Viji ended up together. Viji explained that after breaking up with Jai, she decided to follow her parents' wishes. Since Kathi had no parents, her family found him and arranged their marriage. They shared their past, accepted their situations, and got married. The reunion after fifteen years made them all happy. Eventually, they decided to merge their companies and share profits equally.

As the business grew, they needed to hire two more workers. Jai invited Ram to join the business and hired Merry, a woman who couldn't speak but was a topper in her class.

One day, Jayram and Annapoorani received their first test marks, both scoring between 15 and 18 out of 20. Their teachers praised them, but when they told Swetha, she said, "Good job, but you can do even better." The children were upset and asked Jai why she had responded that way.

Jai explained, "People who want to stop you from succeeding will only say good things. But those who truly love you will also point out areas where you can improve." The children mentioned that one of their friends had copied answers and scored 19/20. Swetha explained, "If he got high marks without hard work, next time he will struggle. Success without effort does not last. Also, a mistake is something you do unknowingly, but doing something wrong despite knowing better is a choice."

As they continued working hard, the business became profitable again. Jai and Swetha invited everyone to their home for a weekend party. They all enjoyed themselves and shared life updates. Divya expressed that despite their wealth, her family was unhappy because they had no children to bring them joy. Meanwhile, Surya, Ram, and Merry were still unmarried. The grandparents advised them to believe in God and trust that everything happens for a reason.

As they returned home, Kathi, Viji, Viji's parents, and Surya travelled in one car, while Divya, her husband, and Merry followed in another. Tragically, Kathi's car met with an accident. Kathi and Viji's parents passed away, Surya lost his hearing, and Viji was severely injured.

Divya witnessed the accident and rushed them to the hospital. Meanwhile, at Jai's house, Jayram asked his father, "How much wealth did you inherit from your parents, and how much did you receive as a dowry from Mom's family?"

Jai replied, "Our parents gave us life, education, and freedom—just as we will give you. They did not give us money or land because they saved it for their needs. If we fail to take care of them or if something happens to us, they should be able to live independently."

At that moment, Jai received a call from Divya about the accident. He, Swetha, and Grandpa rushed to the hospital. While waiting, Divya noticed a three-year-old child crying for food. His parents had also died in a road accident, and his relatives planned to leave him in an orphanage. Divya and her husband asked if they could adopt him, and the relatives agreed. They fed the child and took him home.

When Viji regained consciousness, she learned that her husband and parents had passed away. She cried uncontrollably. Jai felt deep sorrow for his best friend and Surya, who had lost his hearing. He asked his father, "Why did God do this to them?"

His father consoled him, "God has a plan we cannot understand. We must face everything in life with strength."

A few months later, Viji and Surya returned to the business. Viji wanted to forget her past, and Surya needed to earn for his future. When Jai told the family about this, Annapoorani asked how they could overcome such pain. Grandma explained, "It is called interest—when you love something deeply, it changes your mindset."

One day, when only Surya and Merry were in the office, a customer arrived but hesitated to place an order, thinking he should return when others were present. However, Surya and Merry convinced him to stay. The customer explained what he needed, Merry translated it into sign language for Surya, and Surya took the order. Their teamwork was encouraging for everyone.

Later, Divya invited everyone to her son's naming ceremony. During the function, Viji felt emotional, thinking that if Kathi were alive, they too would have children. She tried to hide her pain, but Grandma noticed.

Grandma approached Viji and suggested remarriage, saying, "You are still young and have much to experience in life."

Viji protested, "I lived with Kathi. How can I live with someone else? It would feel like a divorce."

Grandma explained, "It's not wrong. You didn't get divorced—this is simply fate. Change is a constant part of life. We are not forcing you, just asking you to think about it. It is your life, and the choice is yours."

Meanwhile, Surya was working with Merry when he finally admitted, "I have liked you since before my accident. But I never told you because I feared you would think I liked you out of pity. Now, I want you to know that I also have a weakness, and I hope you will consider my feelings."

Merry responded, "I also liked you from the moment I saw you, but I was afraid you would reject me, just like my parents did. When I was born, my parents abandoned me."

Surya reassured her, "I understand that pain. I didn't study well, so my parents scolded me a lot. One day, I ran away and worked as a labourer. Now, I want to spend my life with someone who truly understands me."

Merry replied, "Since I never got to live with my parents, I want to live with yours for the rest of my life. Let's meet them and explain our situation. I hope they will understand."

Jai and Swetha took them to Surya's parents. They were overjoyed to see that their son had become a successful businessman. "We scolded you because we had so many dreams for you. Now, you have fulfilled them," they said, accepting their marriage.

On their wedding day, Jai's mother noticed that Viji was upset, and she asked again about her remarried by mentioning "I asked last time". Viji told Jai's parents, "I am ready for a new life. Please find a suitable person for me."

They introduced her to Ram. Ram hesitated, saying, "I will accept, but I am not a handsome man. Ask her if she is okay with that."

Viji replied, "Beauty is not in appearance; it is in the heart. I like him, and I trust my friend's parents like my parents, who will choose the right person for me."

Viji and Ram were married on the same day as Surya and Merry.

A year later, Surya and Merry and Viji and Ram had children. Life moved forward. Four years later, Divya's son told her he was feeling lonely while his parents were busy with work. She asked Jai and Surya if her child could spend time at their house to play, study, and enjoy life with other children. They agreed.

One day, the children fought with Jayram and Annapoorani and told their parents. The parents advised them, "We will not interfere. Small fights happen in every friendship, so learn to handle them."

The fight lasted for two weeks. Then, Jayram and Annapoorani's birthday arrived. The children had a habit of saving 10 rupees per month from their parents to buy each other gifts. Because of their fight, they hadn't bought anything this time.

The parents worried that their children's friendship wasn't as strong as theirs had been. But to everyone's surprise, the children pooled their savings and gave 200 rupees to Jayram and Annapoorani. "Instead of buying something you may not like, we are giving you this money so you can buy what you truly want," they explained.

Their friendship continued, and all the parents successfully managed their businesses.

Life will continue like this...

Note To Readers:

According to me, life is endless when you have many people around you. If you want, you can shape it as you wish.

• • •

CHAPTER X

TRUE LOVE

In 1998, in Chennai, there lived a married couple—Swami and his wife Chitra. Swami worked a government job, and Chitra was a housewife. They had twin sons named Raju and Siva. However, Swami always wished for a daughter. Four years later, they had a baby girl named Hema. After that, the family lived happily, doing their duties and enjoying holidays together. Swami was a bit strict with the children, while Chitra was more friendly and nurturing.

When the boys completed school, one evening, Swami came home with some snacks, and the whole family sat together, talking.

That day, Swami gave his children advice about society and caste issues. He also spoke about his father, who had served as an Indian Army officer and died for the country.

Swami said, "I had a dream of becoming an army officer, but I failed the final test. That's how I ended up with a government job. I may be strict, but I'll be very happy if even one of you fulfils my dream."

The boys smiled. Life went on as usual.

One day, they went to watch a movie. In the story, the hero was an army officer who had married for love without his parents' support. He died in the final scene, and the government honoured him with a gold medal, compensation, a government job for a family member, and national pride.

On the way back home, Raju and Siva discussed the movie in the car.

Raju said, "I admire the hero. He gave his life for the country. I want to become an army officer too."

Siva replied, "I didn't like it. After the hero died, who took care of his wife and children?"

Raju thought for a moment and realised Siva had a point.

After that, they returned to their usual college routines and studied well.

In April 2018, after college hours, Swami enrolled his sons in a gym and encouraged them to take the army entrance exam. They agreed to try.

One day, while returning home from the gym, Siva told Raju, "I'm doing this just to satisfy Dad. I don't want to join the army. I want to stay with our family."

Raju responded, "I truly want to take the exam. Within two months, I hope to become an army officer and serve the nation."

The exam results came out the next month. Raju was selected, but Siva wasn't. Swami and Chitra were proud of Raju and encouraged him to join the army. Raju was thrilled. Siva told their parents, "I'd like to find a job here in Chennai and stay with you." They agreed.

The family helped Raju pack his bags, as he was to be stationed in Jammu and Kashmir starting the next month.

In **June**, Raju arrived at his assigned army office and began his duties. His senior officer, Major Mohammed, was an excellent leader and had been assigned to guide the new batch. One of his first instructions was,

"Start writing a personal diary. We never know if we'll see our families again. If we do, great. But if not, at least your diary will tell them how you felt and what you went through here."

Raju took the advice seriously. On the first page, he wrote about Major Mohammed and why he was starting the diary.

Raju performed his duties well and showed great discipline. At one point, he asked Major Mohammed the same question Siva had once asked about the movie: "Who will take care of the soldier's family if he dies?"

Major Mohammed's reply deeply impressed Raju, and he recorded it in his diary.

Meanwhile, back in Chennai, Siva had joined a multinational company and was doing well. He continued to go to the gym, as he liked staying fit. Hema was now in the 11th grade and was studying well. She had a good friendship with a boy named Ravi, and both were focused on their academics.

In **August 2018**, Raju had a holiday every alternate Sunday. He made a habit of visiting a nearby temple, followed by lunch at a Tamil restaurant. At this restaurant, he met a girl named **Rani**, who worked there.

The first time he ordered food, she served him, and they spoke briefly in Tamil. Raju was surprised and pleased that she knew the language. From then on, he visited the hotel every alternate Sunday after payday and spent time with Rani. She worked hard, and the hotel owner allowed them to talk freely.

Over time, they shared many personal stories. One Sunday, Rani surprised Raju with a handmade gift. Raju smiled and said,

"I'm going back to Tamil Nadu in January for Pongal. When I return, I'll bring you a gift. That's a promise."

Rani replied, "I'll be waiting."

On **December 30th**, Raju reached Chennai. His family was overjoyed. They celebrated the **New Year 2019** with great enthusiasm.

On New Year's Day, Hema wished Ravi, and they spent some fun moments together. Raju shared stories with his family about Major Mohammed and his new friend Rani. When the family went shopping for Pongal celebrations, Raju also picked out a new dress for Rani. His parents trusted his intentions and allowed it.

They had a wonderful Pongal celebration. During the holidays, Raju didn't write in his diary.

On **February 12th, 2019**, Raju's parents showed him a photo of a girl they had chosen for marriage and asked if he liked her, so they could arrange the wedding during his next leave. Raju said firmly, "Please stop talking about this topic."

His parents asked, "Are you looking for someone more beautiful?"

Raju responded, "Stop talking nonsense. I believe everyone is beautiful in their own way. Beauty isn't in our control—it's God's creation. We don't ask God for fair or dark skin. But I'm not ready for marriage."

Finally, they asked, "Why not?"

Raju quietly said, "Because I'm in love."

His parents were shocked and assumed that he was in love with Rani, the girl he had bought the dress for. Swami became furious and shouted,

"Get out of this house! We don't want to see you again. Don't come back!"

He didn't give Raju a chance to explain. Chitra was heartbroken and cried over her son's "misbehaviour." Raju, deeply hurt, immediately rescheduled his return ticket for that same night. He packed his things into two bags and left the house silently.

Siva was speechless during the confrontation. Hema, who had gone to school, came back and asked about her brother. The family told her that Raju had received an emergency call from his army base and had to leave immediately.

On the train to Delhi, Raju was joined by some of his army friends returning from leave. As the train moved, Raju began writing in his diary again, capturing the painful events of February 12.

On the **morning of February 14ᵗʰ**, Raju and his friends arrived at the Delhi railway station. From there, two army vehicles were arranged to take them to the base.

All their luggage was loaded into the first vehicle, and some officers, including a few of Raju's friends, got into it. Raju, however, boarded the second vehicle with a few others.

As the first vehicle passed a traffic signal, the second was held up. The soldiers in the second vehicle joked and laughed, helping Raju temporarily forget the pain from home.

Suddenly, a van parked next to their vehicle **exploded** in a massive blast. Everyone in the second vehicle died instantly.

Within minutes, every news channel flashed the breaking headline:

"Pulwama Attack in Delhi—Dozens of Soldiers Martyred"

Two days later, Raju's body was brought home, wrapped in the Indian flag—along with his two bags, a **gold medal from the Indian government**, and some compensation. His family was shattered.

Siva placed Raju's bags in his room, unable to bear opening them.

Though life seemed impossible to continue, the family had no choice but to move forward. After about a month, things returned to a semblance of normalcy—on the outside. But Raju was never forgotten.

Swami and Chitra later found a girl named Anu for Siva's marriage, and he agreed. The wedding was set for **April 1ˢᵗ**. Hema invited Ravi to attend her brother's wedding, and he came.

The marriage went well, and everyone was happy—but deep inside, Chitra still carried a silent sorrow for her lost son.

In **May**, Siva and Anu's lives were going smoothly. However, their bedroom was small, so they asked Swami and Chitra if they could move into Raju's room, which was larger. Their parents agreed, saying, "It's your wish."

One late night, while cleaning Raju's room, Siva discovered **Raju's diary and laptop** tucked inside a bag. They moved into the room, and life continued. Later, Anu became **pregnant**.

After **nine months**, in **January 2020**, Anu gave birth to a baby, bringing immense joy to the entire family. They celebrated the arrival of the new member with happiness and renewed hope.

One day, Ravi told Hema,

"This is our final year of school. On **February 13**[th], we'll have our farewell. That day, I want to talk to you about something important."

Ravi also shared with his friends,

"I love Hema, and I'm going to tell her at the farewell."

His friends cheered him on, saying, "Super!"

Meanwhile, **Siva** came home and informed the family that his company had terminated him for certain reasons. He would continue for one more month but would then need to find a new job. Swami advised him calmly,

"This is normal in life. Keep searching—you'll find something better."

In the **first week of February**, Siva stayed at home and began searching for new opportunities.

On the morning of **February 12**[th], Hema had a study holiday and was preparing for exams in the hall. Chitra and Anu were having breakfast, and Swami returned from his morning walk, sitting on the sofa with a cup of tea.

Then, Siva emerged from his room, **dressed in an army uniform with his name stitched on it**. Holding his baby & his brother's army bag, he handed the child to Swami and gathered everyone in the hall.

"I'm in love," Siva said.

Everyone was confused.

Swami asked, "Do you even know what you're saying?"

Siva nodded and held up **Raju's diary and laptop**.

"I started reading Raju's diary. I wanted to know about the love story he once mentioned. And now, I understand. Now, I'm in love with my brother's dreams, his sacrifice, and his life."

He began reading Raju's words from the diary.

On the **first page**, Raju had written about Major Mohammed and why he began journaling.

"If anything ever happens to me, I want my family and friends to know what I experienced after joining the army."

On the **second page**, Raju had answered the question Siva once asked about the movie hero's death. Major Mohammed had told him:

"If everyone thinks only about their families, who will protect the country? If no one saves the nation, eventually it will affect our families too. I understand the fear—if we die, who will take care of our loved ones? But I strongly believe that our Indian brothers and sisters will."

On the **third page**, Raju described how he spent alternate Sundays with **Rani**.

Rani works at a hotel and lives a humble life. She goes to church every Sunday and spends her free time doing handicrafts. We became friends through our shared language—Tamil. In August, she surprised me with something I'll never forget. I promised to bring her a gift from Tamil Nadu."

Siva turned to the **fourth page**, with goosebumps, he showed everyone a **handmade Raksha Bandhan** tied to the page with Rani's name on it.

Raju had bought the dress for Rani as a **sister**, not a lover.

Siva then said,

"That's when I realised how wrong we had judged him. I kept reading."

On the **fifth page**, written during his train journcy, Raju expressed his heartbreak:

"I fought with my family and left. No one asked who I truly loved. My love is not a person—**it's my job, my country, and my family.**

I don't want to leave behind a grieving wife, like in that movie. That's why I've chosen not to marry. I hope one day my family understands." Then Siva shared Raju's definition of love:

I – I AM
L – LIVING
O – ORIGINAL
V – VALUE
E – EMOTIONS / ENJOY
Y – YOUTH
O – OPENNESS
U – UNDERSTAND ME

After hearing this, Swami was overwhelmed with guilt.
"I'm the one who killed my son," he whispered.

The family comforted him.

Then Siva stood and declared,
"I'm going to join the army. I want to serve my country, and I want to deliver Raju's gift to Rani."

Swami asked, "How is that even possible? How will you find Rani? How will you join the army now?"

Siva replied,
"I learned all this eight months ago. I contacted Major Mohammed and told him I wanted to join. He encouraged me to take the army exam online—I passed. I resigned from my job last month. Major Mohammed even mailed me this army uniform to my office. I kept it hidden in my laptop bag. I've seen pictures of Raju's friends, Mohammed Sir, and Rani on his laptop."

Chitra asked tearfully,
"But now, we've already lost one son. How can we let you go too? And what about your wife? How will she live without you?"

Before Siva could answer, Anu spoke up:
"I already know everything. Siva told me the full story. I'm the one who pushed him to follow this path. Raju was the true hero of our family. If Siva sacrifices himself for the nation, I'll raise our son on my own. I have my education—I'll get a job. And if our son wants to join the army one day, I'll proudly let him go."

Then Hema said,

"Like both my brothers, I want to serve our country too. After my studies, I'll join the Défense forces."

Siva gently advised her,

"Women can join the army, but I recommend you join the **Air Force or Navy**. It's a bit safer, and you'll still serve the nation."

The family agreed to support Siva's decision.

He kissed his baby's forehead, received blessings from his parents, and left home with courage in his heart.

On **February 13**[th], Hema went to her school's farewell event. But she was visibly upset. Ravi noticed and asked her what was wrong.

Hema replied, "I just found out everything... about Raju and Siva. I want to study hard and be like both—serve my country."

Ravi said with a smile, "You can do it. I'll always support you. All the best for your future."

After Hema left, Ravi's friends came to him excitedly.

"Did you tell Hema that you love her?"

Ravi shook his head. "No. I couldn't."

His friends scolded him, "Why not? That's their problem. You should just tell her!"

But Ravi got serious and replied,

"You think true love means going on dates, exchanging gifts, hanging locks on a 'promise bridge,' or living together before marriage. But that's not true love. Wasn't Raju's love true?"

His friends were silent.

Ravi continued,

"True love isn't about success or outcome—it's about how genuinely you feel. Even if I confess and she doesn't accept it, I won't act like some guys—getting drunk, angry, or blaming her. I'll continue working hard and being her friend. Maybe one day she'll realise I was right for hcr, maybe not. Either way, my love is real. I love myself first—and then her."

His friends apologised.

"You're right, Ravi. We misunderstood."

Ravi nodded.

"My love and Raju's love are both **one-sided**, but they're not fake. From now on, I'll support Hema in achieving her dreams. I'll work hard, and we'll see where life takes us."

On **February 14th**, Siva reached the army camp and officially joined his unit. He asked for permission to meet **Rani** and tell her everything.

When he found her at the hotel, he gently told her about Raju's passing and handed her the dress Raju had promised.

Rani broke down, crying uncontrollably.

Siva comforted her, saying,

"All of India are brothers and sisters. So now, I'll be your brother. I'll visit you on Sundays like Raju did, and we'll talk and laugh just like old times."

Rani smiled through her tears.

Siva returned to camp. As he passed the Indian flag, he stopped and **saluted** it for two minutes. At that moment, Major Mohammed saw him.

With emotion in his voice, Mohammed said,

"When I saw you stand there, Siva, I saw **Raju's soul** in you. From now on, think of me as your elder brother. If you need anything, just ask."

Siva replied, "Thank you, sir. Jai Hind."

He stood in silence, reflecting.

"Last year, this date was a black day for the nation," he thought.

"But today, it's a colourful one—because I'm a Hindu, my commanding officer is a Muslim, and my sister Rani is a Christian. This is the true power of India's love."

Continues...

Note to the Readers:

This story can end in multiple ways. Choose the one you believe fits best:

A) Siva survives and retires from the army. Hema joins the Navy or the Air Force. She marries Ravi. Ravi becomes successful, and

Siva's son grows up to do what he loves.

B) Siva survives and retires. Hema joins the Navy or Air Force but doesn't marry Ravi. Ravi still becomes successful and remains her close friend. Siva's son follows his passion.

C) Siva dies in a future war. Anu gets a job and raises their son alone. Hema works in a field she feels supports the nation's growth. She marries Ravi. Siva's son joins the army, inspired by his father.

D) You, the reader, can imagine a different ending.

THE END

Author's Note:

Life is unpredictable, and stories—like love and sacrifice—don't always follow one path.

I still remember the real **Pulwama Attack**, which happened on **14-02-2019**. This story is dedicated to the true heroes of India. Please check and remember the history.

• • •

CHAPTER XI

SWEET DREAMS

Babu, a boy studying in the 5th grade, had always studied well up to the 4th grade. One day, he dreamed that he became the first in his class. The next morning, he told his parents about the dream. His father advised him, "It's good to dream like this. Dr. A.P.J. Abdul Kalam Sir always said to dream about what you want to become. But remember, without action, dreams won't come true."

Babu replied, "I'll try my best." He studied very well, and eventually, his dream came true. His life was going well.

Two years later, on 25th March 2019, Babu had another dream. This time, he saw himself dying in an accident on 27th March while returning from school. The next morning, he told his parents, filled with fear that it might happen. His parents tried to calm him down, but he wouldn't listen. So, they took him to a psychiatrist and explained everything.

Psychiatrist: "It's not a big issue. Like everyone else, you're also getting dreams. They may or may not come true. Dreams are often just our wishes or fears."

Babu: "Then how can I stop bad dreams? How can I live a happy life?"

Psychiatrist: "You can manage this in two ways:

1. If you have a bad dream, wake up suddenly — the dream will fade.
2. Since you dreamed of dying in an accident tomorrow, be very careful. Let your father drop and pick you up from school. Sometimes, what we don't dream of happens, and what we do dream of doesn't.

And for your second question, do whatever makes you happy, be a better person, and never hurt others. My advice is: don't share your dreams with others in ways that create fear like this again."

Babu followed the advice. The next day, he avoided the accident.

Later, when he was in the 9th grade, he started liking his classmate Durga, who was also a top student. He planned to express his feelings after the 10th exams, where he scored over 95%. But when he told her, she said she was already in a relationship and would be attending the same school as her boyfriend for 11th grade.

Babu was heartbroken. That night, he dreamed he was trying to rape Durga. Shocked and disturbed, he woke up, drank water, and thought, "If I do such a thing, it will ruin her life and mine. I'd end up in jail." He decided such thoughts should never occur again.

Later, he had another dream — this time about committing suicide. Again, he woke up and thought, "If I die, who will take care of my parents? They are my whole life." He washed his face, prayed to God to stop the dreams, and then slept peacefully.

He continued his studies, scored above 80% in the 11th and 12th, and joined college. He felt a bit more relaxed. One day, he attended a birthday party with his parents and saw a girl named Sugee, a first-year medical student. At first, he thought she wouldn't like him.

But their parents introduced them as family friends, and soon Babu and Sugee became close and exchanged WhatsApp numbers. They began chatting daily.

As they grew closer, Babu thought, "Why not try love again?" He believed love motivated him to do well. During the first semester, he studied while staying connected with Sugee and scored above 90%.

One day, he invited her to a park and confessed his love. He also shared his ambition to become an IAS officer. But Sugee replied, "I have no experience in love, and I'm afraid it might ruin our studies. I'm also not sure if our parents would accept it. If it's in our fate, we'll be together."

Babu replied, "Okay. But my love is one-sided. You can't stop someone from loving." Sugee answered, "That's your hope. I can't say anything about it."

That evening, he held onto a little hope because she hadn't said no. He decided he would propose again if he passed the IAS exam.

Meanwhile, Sugee saw a family photo that included Babu and felt emotional, realising she also loved him.

That night, Babu had another dream: he finished his college degree with high marks, moved to Delhi to prepare for the IAS exam, maintained his love for Sugee, and waited for results. But just when he was about to see his results in the dream, his parents woke him up.

Time flew. He finished college and joined an IAS coaching centre in Delhi for six months. Sugee became a doctor and worked in a hospital. They continued chatting daily. When his exams neared, Sugee messaged, "All the best, da." That message motivated him, and he did well.

After his exams, he told his parents, "I'll take the train today (Monday) and reach Tamil Nadu by Wednesday. The IAS results will be out on Friday."

His parents spoke privately. His mother said, "He's 25 now. We should look for a bride." His father replied, "Yes. And if he passes the exam, he'll soon be an IAS officer. I know a perfect girl —

Sugee."

On Tuesday evening, they visited Sugee's house and proposed the marriage. Her parents happily agreed. When Sugee returned from work, her mother spoke to her privately. Later, Sugee came out and told everyone, "What happened before, and I know he'll pass just like he did on the 10th. I want to propose to him after the result, with all your blessings." Everyone agreed and planned the engagement for that evening at Babu's house.

Babu came home on Wednesday and prepared to propose. On Friday at 10 a.m., he checked the result and saw he had passed the IAS exam. He excitedly informed his thrilled parents. He tried calling Sugee, but she didn't answer. Just then, the doorbell rang — it was Sugee and her family.

Babu shared the news. Her father said, "Great! We came here because today is her engagement in the evening." Sugee had taken leave from work. They went shopping for the ceremony, leaving both at Babu's home.

Afterwards, Babu went to his room and cried, realising this might be his only chance to propose. He gathered courage and came to the hall — but before he could say anything, Sugee told him, "I love you, with a ring. I want to marry you."

He was speechless. Their parents entered the home by clapping. With tears in his eyes, Babu listened as Sugee explained everything. Within three months, they were married.

After marriage, they lived happily in Babu's house. One day, both had a dream — this time about their future together.

Dreams will continue...

THE END

Note to Reader:

I wish all your good dreams come true and all your bad dreams disappear — just like in this story.

● ● ●

CHAPTER XII

Art and Artist

Arjun was born into a middle-class family. His father, Ashok, worked as an engineer in a private company, while his mother, Anitha, was a company secretary in a government organisation. They spent one-third of their total salary and tried to save the remaining two-thirds in the bank & With her knowledge of trade, Anitha invested some of their savings in mutual funds with Ashok's approval.

Arjun was in the 7th grade. He was an average student in academics, sports, and extracurricular activities, especially music. He was part of the school music group as a singer.

Ashok was worried about his son because he had been an average student. Ashok had failed to pass the CAT exam even after four attempts. Ashok strongly believed that only education could help a person lead a successful and happy life. He came from a poor background and had always dreamt of going to the USA to advance his career. On the other hand, Anitha believed both education and extracurricular activities were equally important, like the two hands of a person. Losing either one would limit a person's ability.

She decided to find out which area Arjun was stronger in before he completed 8th grade. She planned to help him focus primarily on his strength while not completely neglecting the other. If one didn't work out, he could shift to the other later.

Every night, after finishing their chores, the family would spend time together watching TV programs or the news. One night, while watching the news, Arjun got excited and shouted, "Please don't change the channel!" The news was about D. Gukesh winning the 2024 World Chess Championship at age 18.

Ashok said dismissively, "Very few succeed. Why waste time on art or sports? Why are you so happy about someone winning a chess championship?" Arjun and Anitha were shocked. They didn't realise Ashok was against all forms of art, though they kept quiet.

That winter, starting December 14, Arjun had school holidays. He and Anitha went to their village, where they met Subbu—Anitha's nephew, who was pursuing an MBA while working part-time at a call centre. During a walk, Arjun asked Subbu how he spent his free time. Subbu said he enjoyed making TikTok videos with his friends.

A month later, they returned to Chennai.

One day, Anitha received a message on Instagram from her childhood best friend Priya. She now lives in Singapore with her husband. Priya messaged:

"You missed my wedding due to your CS final exams, and I missed yours because I left for Singapore after mine. I found you on Instagram. We're travelling to the UAE this Saturday, December 21. We'll be at Chennai airport for a five-hour layover. Can we meet there with our families?"

Anitha agreed and saved the number Priya sent of her husband.

That Saturday, Ashok drove them to the airport. On the way, he told Anitha, "My friends in the UAE are buying a big lottery ticket. Maybe Priya's husband can help us buy one too." Anitha said she'd ask later.

As they drove, a folk song played on the radio. Ashok asked Arjun about his village trip. Arjun mentioned Subbu and said, "He acted well. I saw his TikTok video!" Ashok responded harshly, "This generation is irresponsible. They just waste time on things like that."

Arjun stayed silent.

Near the airport, Anitha tried calling Priya's husband, but the signal was poor. Arjun suggested trying WhatsApp since many people connect to free airport Wi-Fi. Ashok agreed. When Anitha saw the WhatsApp profile, it said, **"Driving is art."** She told them.

Ashok laughed and joked, "Then everyone should learn driving and become artists!" Anitha scolded him, "You haven't even met him. Why make fun?" Ashok replied, "It was just a joke, don't be upset."

Suddenly, a truck in front of their car braked, and Ashok had to stop abruptly to avoid a crash. Arjun warned, "Drive safely!" Ashok muttered, "It's the truck driver's fault..."

They reached the airport. Anitha and Arjun went inside, while Ashok parked the car. He heard on FM radio that due to a change in the US presidential election, all prior agreements between India and the US had been cancelled, and investments would decline. He felt regret about investing in mutual funds. Anitha also received the same news on her CS WhatsApp group.

They met Priya's family. The friends caught up, and Priya introduced her husband as a pilot who also loved car racing. He was taking annual leave to compete in the Dubai 24H sports car race on January 12, 2025. Priya asked, "Where's your husband?" Anitha said, "He's parking the car."

When Ashok arrived, Priya was shocked—it was her college classmate! She said aloud, "You used to be such a creative writer! I thought you'd become a movie director or author. Your ideas were so original, even though your English wasn't great."

Ashok cut in, "Please stop. You don't know what happened in my life, and I don't want to explain." He asked Anitha and Arjun to come with him. Anitha apologised to Priya, and they left.

Back in the car, Ashok, with tears in his eyes, said, "Please don't ask me about it. That part of my life is gone." Anitha shouted, "We have a right to know! Why are you killing the artist in you?" Arjun begged, "Please tell us. Maybe we can help."

Ashok explained, "As Priya said, I loved writing stories. Some encouraged me, but others mocked my English. Some close friends even refused to read my work. I felt it was all a waste of time and too risky, so I gave up. I programmed my mind to believe that only education matters."

Arjun said, "You asked me why I was happy about Gukesh's win. I believe that if we celebrate others' success, our success will come true, and others will be happy. You let a few people ruin your passion. Creativity is more important than perfect English."

Anitha added, "You kept trying the CAT exam four times but gave up writing so easily?"

Ashok admitted, "I never really invested in myself."

Anitha smiled, "The most powerful weapon for ordinary people is **time**. Why not invest some of it in yourself? Like Priya's husband, use weekends or holidays to pursue your passion. If you can believe in a lottery, why not believe in yourself?"

Ashok replied, "Even if I try, who'll fund a movie or publish my book?"

Anitha said, "You don't know what's happening with our investments..." Ashok sighed, "Even if I write, it's full of grammar mistakes. Who'll want to work with me?" Arjun said, "Use Grammarly app! And find people like you—like Subbu, who also works in his free time."

Ashok said, "Easier said than done. Still, I'll think about it overnight."

The next morning, Ashok said, "I'll try. I'll release a short film on YouTube for my birthday." Anitha and Arjun were thrilled. Ashok asked Subbu if they could collaborate on a low-budget movie. Subbu agreed to ask his friends.

By the weekend, they had a team—including a theatre owner—but no editor. Arjun suggested posting on social media. Anitha hesitated, asked how we could believe that unknown person, so Subbu smiled and asked many people to deposit their money in Yes Bank, but they ran off without him. Anitha said that there is the RBI Act and other Acts, so they will be taken care of. Subbu replies that so we could agree with the editor., So she was convinced.

Soon, they got a message on Instagram from Arnavi Sharma, a young editor from Delhi.

Ashok called the number; an old man answered, saying he was Arnavi's father. "My child is busy but very talented. Share the agreement and footage, and Arnavi will handle everything."

Anitha worried they might demand more later. Subbu suggested a clear contract allowing only this one condition. Everyone agreed.

The next 3 months were filled with shooting, editing, and dubbing. On May 2, they submitted the film to the CBFC. On May 27, they received a U/A certificate for their film "V.M. Krishna." The review noted 5% adult content but approved it for its strong social message.

Their film was scheduled to release on June 12, with three showtimes. The theatre owner warned that if fewer than 50% of seats were filled in the first two shows, the third would be cancelled.

With little money left for promotion, Ashok prayed for help. That evening, a CBFC reviewer named Balu visited and gifted Ashok ₹5,000, praising the film. Ashok used part of the money to distribute free passes to the press and cast members and arranged a press meeting.

At the event, journalists praised the editing and asked questions about the story and themes. Ashok explained their goal and journey. The first person says, "I saw a movie that was all very good, but it has a little bit adult concept, but it is necessary to make an impact. My question is, how do families bring their children to this? You might choose another story.

Ashok said that "an answer to your question is in your answer, it is necessary, and nowadays, children are also aware of everything quickly and smartly in their actions and talk in common places and on social media. If you feel that it will affect your children, please don't bring it and ask them to see it after they become adults."

The same person asked Ashok When you send your stories to your friend, what are the motivating words that move you forward?

He smiles & says, "When I wrote 1st story, which has 3 parts, and sent it to my friends & one of my friends asked me all your concepts in this one story and how you get new concepts for new stories. I replied, "I would try my best", so it motivated me a lot. Till now, I have written 12 different stories.

The next person asked for half of the seats as the first show, so what are your further plans if this movie doesn't go well?

That time, an old man came inside and sat on a chair which was reserved for an editor.

If you like this movie, please gift the tickets to your loved ones.

Ashok said we have different jobs, this is like passion, so it is just a try, we are all back to work tomorrow. If I get profits, we can work on more movies or reach a break-even point. I will try to publish books, or if they are a loss, then I will tell my stories to my grandchildren as bedtime stories.

Another person asked why you were saying the diplomatic answer. Subbu smiles first and said I will answer it "According to my knowledge there are only 3 types of answers those are **Positive, Diplomatic or negative answers** if we give positive answers, you may say we are overconfident we can't say negative about our work, then what you want us to answer, so the director told like it.

One journalist mocked the editor's absence. Just then, an old man (the father of the editor) appeared. In his speech, he revealed that Arnavi was a transgender person and faced social stigma, which is why she never came out.

Anitha declared, "From now on, your child will be known only as an *artist*."

A reporter called it a drama, Ashok got tense and asked, ok, we all are doing drama, but an hour before one of your friends applied, our editor was also drama, ha? Please stop liking this comment. If I say today our national youngest chess player, Anish Sarkar, may win our First India chess grandmaster, Viswanathan Anand, you will say it is also drama to support the youngest one, but first, please understand that when we love art and art, it will love us back. So, as I said before, if I direct the next movie or if I publish a book, your child will be editing or designing the book. So, they give payment to all artists who work in their movies.

After the movie's success, Ashok got a message from an old friend who finally appreciated his story. The second show had 65% attendance, and reviews online were positive.

That night, the team celebrated. At the airport, they dropped off Arnavi's father and returned home.

Ashok turned to Anitha and said, "Now I realise—having a stable job while pursuing art on the side is a *smart*, not a foolish, choice."

Arjun grinned, "Let's take a selfie!"

The next morning, Ashok woke up, happy and refreshed. But when he checked the date, it was December 22. Everything had been a dream.

THE END

Note to Readers:

Like Ashok, are we making excuses? Or will we finally take one real step to bring out our inner artist? I've realised my art—this is my first book of 12 inspiring stories.

• • •